D1302923

Little Eaglet

Loses Her Feathers

Darlene W. Hatcher

Illustrated by Christopher Waner

insight *i* publishing group

Tulsa, Oklahoma

LITTLE EAGLET LOSES HER FEATHERS

Little Eaglet Loses Her Feathers by Darlene W. Hatcher
Published by Insight Publishing Group
8801 S. Yale, Suite 410
Tulsa, OK 74137
918-493-1718

This book or parts thereof may not be reproduced in any form, stored in a retrieval system, or transmitted in any form by any means—electronic, mechanical, photocopy, recording, or otherwise—without prior written permission of the publisher, except as provided by United States copyright law.

Text copyright © 2002 by Darlene W. Hatcher

Illustrations copyright © 2002 by Christopher Waner

All rights reserved

ISBN 1-930027-55-9
Library of Congress catalog card number: 2002105045

Printed in the United States of America

A Note from the Author

*The staff at Eagle Vision Industries hopes
that Little Eaglet will touch your
heart with her enthusiasm
and love for life.*

*Little Eaglet's character lives on in many
other adventures as she discovers life.*

*We enjoy sharing her hope
with young people who
represent tomorrow's generation.*

Eagle Vision Industries
5011 Mountain Air Circle
Colorado Springs, CO 80916

Phone: (719) 380-7338
Email: dlittleeaglet@aol.com

Little Eaglet really enjoyed school. She loved her teacher Ms. Lorraine. They were learning about the mountain where they lived—how to tell which berries were okay to eat, which ones were poisonous, what sounds to listen for, and what dangers to avoid.

Ms. Lorraine was also teaching the class of eaglets how to build a nest, which kinds of branches and twigs were the strongest and which feathers were the warmest.

L ittle Eaglet was so proud to share her own personal adventure in nest building. She was the main attraction, explaining to the whole class how she and her mom built their nest. The eaglets beamed with admiration as she told them about the thread that held their nest together. She was so excited about her day and how popular she was that she couldn't wait to get home to share it with her mom, Eagle.

Little Eaglet felt so happy and carefree as she walked along the path that she didn't even notice she was losing a few feathers. It was a very warm day, with no breeze blowing to keep her cool. Already hot and tired from her journey, she stopped by the small stream to rest under a shade tree.

Perched on the bank of a stream looking at her reflection, she suddenly screeched, "Oh No! Oh My! What is going on? What is happening to me? What happened to my feathers? They're *gone*!"

Exasperated, Little Eaglet started flapping her wings in a frenzy saying, "Where are my feathers? What happened to my feathers? What am I going to do? I can't fly without feathers!"

She looked back at the path where she had been walking and squawked when she saw her feathers lying on the ground. Totally upset, she again fluttered her wings, this time with big tears rolling down her cheeks as she peeped, "I'm never going to soar like Eagle. How will I ever fly again without my feathers?"

Little Eaglet was so sad. She started thinking out loud, "If I can never soar with Eagle, then maybe she won't like me anymore. I can't go home."

Little Eaglet felt so down and alone that all she wanted to do was sit by the water's edge and cry. She didn't know that someone had been watching her the whole time. The little creature slowly moved closer to Little Eaglet, trying not to be noticed. But Little Eaglet's eyes were becoming very sharp. The little creature jumped when Little Eaglet spotted him. She motioned for him to come closer. "Who are you?" she exclaimed.

"My name is Oscar," replied the bunny. He was dressed in faded overalls, wearing an old red cap that sat between his floppy ears. He boldly asked, "Why are ya cryin'?"

Little Eaglet took a deep breath before answering, "I've lost my feathers. I'll never be able to fly and now I can't go home."

Oscar scratched his floppy ear, not quite understanding Little Eaglet's problem and said, "You can come to my home with me."

"Where do you live?" inquired Little Eaglet.

"I live in that great big oak tree over there," replied Oscar.

Little Eaglet said with a chirp, "I live at the top of *that* big oak tree. Eagle and I built our nest up there. You'll have to meet Eagle. She is so nice, and I love her so much."

Stumped, Oscar asked, "If your mom is so nice and you love her so much, then why can't you go home?"

"I lost my feathers!" Little Eaglet exclaimed, spreading her wings as she continued, "I can't even go to school; my friends will laugh at me. Look how ugly I am."

Oscar began to understand how much Little Eaglet was upset and comforted her by saying, "It's okay, I'll be your friend. I don't think you're ugly. I think you're very pretty."

Little Eaglet looked at Oscar and softly asked, "You want to be my friend?"

Oscar's ears perked straight up, he smiled and said, "Oh yeah! I don't have many friends. I just have brothers and sisters."

"Wow!" exclaimed Little Eaglet, "How many brothers and sisters do you have?"

"I have seven brothers and five sisters, and I'm the youngest," replied Oscar.

Meanwhile, at the top of the big oak tree, Eagle was waiting for Little Eaglet to come home. School had been out for a long time and she had never been this late before. Eagle decided to search for Little Eaglet, so she flew over the schoolyard, but she was not there. Next, Eagle checked by the stream, since it was one of Little Eaglet's favorite places to play. As Eagle was flying above the path that Little Eaglet had walked earlier, she noticed all the feathers lying along the trail. "Now I know," Eagle said to herself as she continued looking for Little Eaglet.

While Little Eaglet and Oscar were talking, his mom called him home for dinner. "I have to go now," Oscar said, "but you're welcome to come home with me. We're having carrot soup."

Little Eaglet paused for a moment, "Thank you Oscar, but I think I'll just stay here by the stream for a while."

Oscar hopped along the path to his house, glad to have made a new friend. Turning around just before he was out of sight, he hollered, "I'll see you again Little Eaglet! Goodnight!"

L ittle Eaglet looked back into the stream at her reflection and thought out loud, "I miss Eagle. I bet she has a basket of fresh berries waiting for me at home. I sure am hungry. What am I going to do? I can't go home, I don't have any feathers." Just as Little Eaglet was finishing her sentence, Eagle squawked as she swooped down to the stream's edge.

L ittle Eaglet was so excited, "Eagle! What are you doing here?"

Eagle looked at Little Eaglet and wrapped her wings around her tightly and whispered in her ear, "It's all right. I'm here now."

Relieved that Eagle was there, Little Eaglet cried, "I've lost my feathers. What am I going to do? What's wrong with me?"

Eagle nestled close to her and explained how eagles lose their feathers when they are young. She told her how beautiful, strong, and sleek her new ones would be in a few days.

"Really!" exclaimed Little Eaglet.

"Yes." Eagle answered with confidence.

"Oh no!" cried Little Eaglet, "I can't go to school tomorrow. All my friends will laugh at me. I will feel so embarrassed."

Eagle chuckled, "You *must* go to school, and no one will laugh at you, I promise."

"You promise?" Little Eaglet asked.

"Yes, I promise." Eagle replied with a smile.

As Little Eaglet climbed on Eagle's back for the flight home she asked, "Will I be able to soar with my new feathers?"

"Yes," answered Eagle, adding, "but first you must shed your feathers two more times. With each time you lose your eaglet feathers, your new eagle feathers will become stronger and with that strength, you will be able to soar high above any storm that comes."

W hen they landed in the nest, Little Eaglet was still unhappy about having to shed feathers two more times. "Two more times! I have to lose my feathers two more times?!"

Eagle didn't answer as they settled into the nest for the night. Little Eaglet carried on until she fell asleep. Eagle tended the fire all through the night to keep Little Eaglet warm.

The next day Little Eaglet came up with a variety of reasons why she couldn't go to school. Finally, after much reassurance from Eagle, she headed out for school.

As she passed by the stream, she saw Oscar on his way to bunny school. He greeted Little Eaglet. "You sure do look pretty this morning."

Little Eaglet smiled really big and said, "Thank you, Oscar."

He continued warmly, "You just remember how pretty you are and don't you listen to anyone who tells you anything different."

L ittle Eaglet was quick to return the compliment, "You're so nice, Oscar. I really like you. You make me feel so good about myself." Then, with a deep sigh, she announced, "Well, I must be on my way."

Before she left, they agreed to meet and play by the stream after school.

Little Eaglet felt confident after hearing Eagle's words of encouragement and seeing Oscar that morning.

Along the path to her school, she saw lots of different feathers that did not belong to her. What a surprise she found when she walked into the classroom! Half of the class had lost their feathers too!

When Ms. Lorraine noticed how many eaglets were without feathers, she changed her lesson plans for the day. She taught the eaglets all about the pain of losing eaglet feathers and the joy of gaining eagle feathers. She told them how strong their new feathers would be each time they went through the process of what she called "molting."

After school, the eaglets gathered together, chirping and exchanging stories of how and where they each noticed their feathers were gone. Even the eaglets who had not lost their feathers yet asked questions about how it felt. They asked, "Did it hurt? Do you feel weird? Aren't you cold?"

Ms. Lorraine watched from the window and was proud to see how all the eaglets were so kind to one another.